999 Abroad

Börkur Sigurbjörnsson

999 Abroad

short fiction

Urban Volcano

999 Abroad
Börkur Sigurbjörnsson
Creative Commons (BY-NC-ND) – 2012
http://creativecommons.org/licenses/by-nc-nd/3.0/

Cover: Börkur Sigurbjörnsson
Illustrations: Yana Volkovich
Publisher: Urban Volcano

http://borkur.net
http://urbanvolcano.net

ISBN 978-9935-9095-3-4

CONTENTS

OF ELVES AND KINGS

I sat down on a bench in Vondelpark. The sun was shining. I wiped sweat from my forehead. I had recently abandoned the Icelandic summer and moved into the Dutch autumn. The autumn being considerably warmer than the summer. I had difficulty coping with the heat. Having lived the first twenty-four years of my life in Iceland, I was not used to this sort of heat.

I sat with a notebook in my lap and a pen in my

hand, with the intention of writing a script for a short film about parklife in Amsterdam. However, my mind was blank. I could not squeeze out a word. The page was equally blank. Was it the heat that caused my writer's block? Or was there too much turmoil going on in my head? Turmoil caused by the recent changes in my life.

I was starting a new chapter in my life. A chapter in which I hoped to become richer in creative content than the empty page in the notebook I had in front of me. It was the first autumn of the new millennium. I had left sparsely populated Iceland behind me and moved to densely populated Netherlands. A few months after finishing a degree in mathematical logic, I was about to start a course in film making. I had left the scientific world behind me and was heading into an imaginary one. It was not the stereotypical educational path.

"Het is nog steeds vrij warm hoor!"

I looked up from my empty notebook to the man who had sat down beside me. Talking about stereotypes. Although I assumed he was a local, he was not what you would call a stereotypical Dutchman – the tall, slim blond – he was short and chubby with sweat running down his bald head. He had sat down beside me to catch his breath. He had been running.

"Sorry, I don't speak any Dutch," I replied in English. I was sure he had said something about it being warm or something, but that was all I had got.

"Oh, I just said it was still warm," the Dutchman repeated, this time in English.

"Yes, it is warm," I agreed.

We sat in silence and watched the life in the park. I with my blank mind. He with his bald head. He trying to catch his breath and squeeze it down into his lungs. I trying to catch the spirit in the park and write it into my script.

"Where are you from?" the Dutchman asked.

"Iceland."

The Dutchman raised his eyebrows, nodding his head looking genuinely surprised.

"Wow. As far as I can recall, this is the first time I have met someone from Iceland," the Dutchman said, still nodding his head as if he was trying to convince himself that he had indeed met a specimen of the rare species known as Icelanders. "Do you know Björk?"

What? I hesitated. What sort of question was that? I knew of course that Björk was famous all over the world, but I still thought it was an odd question. It was like me asking if he knew Ruud Gullit. It was a long shot.

"Well, no. I mean yes, but no," I said awkwardly. "Not personally. Not her."

Of course I knew Björk. My sister's name is Björk. I did not know THE Björk. I only knew a Björk. I did not know the singer. Not personally.

"So it is not true that everybody knows everybody in Iceland?"

"No, not really," I replied thinking of all the Icelandic people I did not know. "It is not even true that most people know most people."

"Huh," was all the Dutchman had to say. He raised his eyebrows and looked a bit disappointed that I had not confirmed the myth about the small and tightly woven social network in Iceland.

"Yet, quite a few people know quite a few people," I continued. "But, ..."

I hesitated and wondered where I was going with this argument. The Dutchman nodded his head and waited for me to continue the thought.

"But I guess the same is true here in the Netherlands," I said grinning. "I mean, here there are even more people that know even more people."

I was rather pleased with my response. I thought it was fairly funny. Well, if not funny then at least witty.

"No, I don't think so," the Dutchman said with a serious face.

We sat in silence. I was a bit taken aback by the Dutchman's lack of response to my wit. Perhaps it had not come out right. Perhaps it had simply not been funny. I hesitated to continue the discussion and decided to go back to my script. Or rather, I went back to the blank piece of paper that was supposed to become my script. I had yet to put the first word onto the page. I looked around the park in search of inspiration. Arguably, I could not get a better source of inspiration for a script about parks in Amsterdam than looking around a park in Amsterdam. Yet I could not get a single word out of my pen.

"But tell me," the Dutchman said, his face lighting up as if he had just remembered something remarkable. "Is it true that Icelandic people believe in elves?"

"Yes," I said hesitantly. I had not anticipated this question either. Was it really elves and Björk that symbolized Iceland in the eyes of the world?

"Really?" the Dutchman said with questioning eyes. "Everybody?"

"No, maybe not everybody," I said and tried to remember if I had ever seen statistics about how many Icelandic people believed in elves. I did not come up with much. I recalled having seen some numbers at some point about the percentage of Icelandic people who believed in elves. However, I could not even remember in which ballpark the percentage was. It was not as if this was a hot topic in Iceland. The pollsters were interested in more serious subjects such as the popular support for the government or whether or not Iceland should join the European Union.

"And you?" the Dutchman asked grinning. "Do you believe in elves?"

I hesitated. For a moment I thought that this question called for some contemplation. I had lived twenty-four years in Iceland without having to make up my mind about whether I believed in elves. The occasion had never arisen. I had never been involved in moving large rocks or tunneling through mountains – the main activities affecting the presumed habitats of elves and thus instigating interaction with them. I did not even know if Iceland should join the European Union. The question about the existence of elves was even farther from my mind.

I felt slightly overwhelmed by the fact that I had to make up my mind. In my life I had not experienced anything that suggested the existence of elves. Yet, neither had I experienced anything that gave me grounds to argue against their existence either. Maybe it was the same with elves as with penguins. Even though I had never seen one, it did not mean that I doubted their existence. Yet, maybe penguins and elves were not comparable. Anyway, I had to make up my mind. I had to answer the Dutchman's question. To believe or not to believe – in elves – that was the question.

"Yes," I replied firmly, more based on instinct rather than conviction. "And the feeling is mutual. Elves believe in me too."

I did not know where the latter statement came from. It was just something that had spontaneously popped into my mind.

"Really?" The Dutchman looked surprised. In a way, I could not blame him. I was quite surprised myself. "But why?"

That was a good question. As my answer had been based on instinct rather than on careful reasoning, I was not prepared to argue my case.

"Why not?" I replied, fully realizing that answering with a question was not a satisfying answer. "Believing in elves causes no harm, and it might be fun."

In my mind I recalled a recent news item I had seen about school children singing for the elves in a reconciliation meeting. Workers had been blowing up rocks on the slopes of a mountain above a fishing village in north-west Iceland. Something went wrong and rock fragments rained down over the village. A school teacher argued that this was the work of the angry elves whose habitat had been destroyed by the explosions. He took his pupils to the construction site and organized a concert where the children sang for the elves. I had thought it was a nice gesture. Regardless of the existence of elves.

"But it makes no sense," the Dutchman replied. "How can you believe in something that does not make any sense?"

I wondered if there was no way of pleasing this guy. First, he seemed disappointed by the fact that I had downplayed the myth about the density of the Icelandic social network. Now, he seemed disappointed that I had confirmed the myth about the Icelanders' belief in elves. I had to try to find a convincing answer. I could play the the penguin card. However, it was possible that the Dutchman had at some point been to South America – or to a zoo. Hence, he might have an easy answer to the question about the existence of the mysterious and supernatural species known as penguins. Thus, I decided to take another route.

"I guess it is a bit like believing in the royal family," I said, immediately realizing that I might have chosen a delicate subject.

"But that's different," the Dutchman exclaimed. "The royal family exists. Believing in elves serves no purpose."

Of course the Dutchman was right in the sense that believing in elves had no functional purpose. Not in our fact-driven and rational modern times, at least. He had however touched a sensitive nerve. For some reason I felt obliged to defend the elves. I felt obliged to defend imagination against functionality. I felt the obligation to defend my current existence against my past. To defend the joy of the imaginary world against the utility of the real one.

"Doesn't the same go for royalty?" I said "Does believing in the royal family have a purpose?"

The Dutchman did not answer right away. I wondered if I had gone too far. Perhaps, discussing the utility of the royal family was a sensitive topic.

"The royal family has a purpose," the Dutchman said after a moment's thought. "The royal family is a unifying symbol of the nation."

I knew that argument well. We used it in Iceland in the context of the Icelandic president. The president whose role was comparable to an elected monarchy.

"But can't elves perform the same function?" I said, still thinking of the role of the Icelandic president. "Can't elves function as the unifying symbols of a nation too?"

I thought that I was on to something. There seemed to be some parallels between seemingly unrelated concepts.

"But also," the Dutchman exclaimed. "The royal family is the symbol of the Netherlands in the eyes of the outside world."

I could not help grinning. The Dutchman had unknowingly given me yet another parallel between elves and kings. As far as I could work out from this discussion, elves – and Björk – symbolized the Icelandic nation in the eyes of the outside world.

"In the case of Iceland," I said with a grin on my face. "Elves symbolize the Icelandic nation in the eyes of the outside world."

I stood up and said goodbye to the running Dutchman. I was off to find another bench where I could elaborate on my current inspiration and write a short film script about the parallels of elves and royalty in our modern society.

THE STORM

I open my eyes and stare at the ceiling. I cannot sleep.
I listen. The wind howls at the window, producing
a soft whistling sound when it tries to make its way
through a crack between the window and the frame.

I close my eyes. The wind blows me thousands
of kilometers north and decades back in time. From
my apartment in Barcelona, over the Atlantic Ocean
and on to a farm on the east coast of Iceland. I sit on

the bed and stare out through the window. I cannot see much because the snowstorm is so dense. I cannot sleep. I enjoy sitting in the warm room and watching the storm dancing outside. There is something about the storm that fascinates me. Its power. Its strength.

I open my eyes. You lie beside me sleeping soundly. You are surrounded by an aura of silence. You look as if you are having a pleasant dream. To you the wind is just a breeze. You don't know about the snowstorm. I have told you stories but you haven't experienced it firsthand. Not yet. Maybe we should travel to Iceland one day in winter. Maybe I should introduce you to the snowstorm.

I close my eyes. My mother enters the room and sits besides me on the bed. Together we watch the storm outside. "Is it the wind?" she asks. "Yes," I reply and I lean my head on her shoulder. She wraps her arm around me and caresses my forehead. "Don't be afraid," she says. "You are safe in here. Now, go to sleep." She lays me carefully onto the bed and forces me to close my eyes with a gentle stroke over my eye-lids. I lie awake with my eyes closed – listening to the storm.

I open my eyes. Two decades by the Mediterranean Sea have not managed to erase from my mind the association between the howling of the wind and the image of the snowstorm. A storm is rare around here. Too rare to blow the association out of my mind. Even as I lie awake and stare at the ceiling I can see the storm. It is snowing in my mind.

I close my eyes. I get out of bed and walk into the living room. My grandmother is sitting in an armchair at the far end of the room. She is knitting. She raises her head and puts the knitting needles aside when I enter. I walk over to her chair. "Is it the wind?" she asks. "Yes," I reply and crawl onto her lap. "Don't be afraid," she says. "You are safe in here. Now, go to sleep." She caresses the back of my head and sings a lullaby. After a while my grandfather picks me up from my grandmother's lap and carries me back to my bed.

I open my eyes. You are awake. You are watching me. I smile to you as if to apologize for being awake. "Is it the wind?" you ask. "Yes," I reply. You move closer and lay your head on my shoulder. "Don't be afraid," you say. "You are safe here in the south. Now, go to sleep." You take my hand and stroke it gently.

I close my eyes. Your aura of silence surrounds me. I listen to the storm, but all I can hear is a breeze. I fall asleep.

WHAT IS THE TRAFFIC LIKE IN FINLAND?

It was a bright and sunny July morning in Barcelona. The sky was blue and there wasn't a cloud in sight. It was hot – unusually hot – but less humid than one would expect for an average July. It was no average July. It was July alright, but outside the mean. To some, it was mean outside – depending on the angle from which one looked at the weather. The city was quiet. The night owls had not yet woken up and the people who ventured outside moved around slowly in order not to exhaust themselves in the heat.

Two men sat at a table on the terrace of a café in Virreina square. They tried to combat the heat by drinking cold beer. Some readers might raise their eyebrows at the idea of drinking beer so early in the morning. As an experienced narrator, I can however testify that I have seen worse behavior, and in the case of those two young gentlemen I can promise the readers that they are decent gentlemen who will not be harmed by a beer or two – even at this early hour. One of the men was dark. He had dark hair, brown eyes, and uniformly tanned skin. Probably a local. The other – despite having eyes whose color perfectly matched the clear blue sky above – did not fit as well into the stereotypical Mediterranean scene. His hair was blond and his skin was white, with a slight hint of pink – most likely caused by the sun rather than the beer. One would have guessed he was Swedish or Norwegian. At least from a place considerably north of the Mediterranean.

A car stopped in the middle of the street that ran along one side of the square. The driver shouted at one of the passers-by.

"¡Ostras crack! ¡Cuanto tiempo!"

The driver got out of the car, ran to the passer-by and hugged him. Apparently they knew each other and had not seen each other for a while. They were happy to see each other. The other drivers however, were not as happy with this encounter and started to honk their horns.

"¡Hombre! ¿Qué pasa?"

The driver stopped hugging the passer-by and shouted to the other drivers that he would be moving on in a minute.

"¡Tranquilos! Continuaré en un minuto."

The other drivers shouted insults back and continued honking their horns. The normally quiet square became noisy. Possibly waking up a night owl or two.

"What is the traffic like in Finland?" asked the man who one would guess was probably a local.

"Iceland?" replied the blond who one would have guessed was either Swedish or Norwegian. "Did you mean to ask what the traffic is like in Iceland?"

"Yes, of course." The local looked surprised. "What else?"

"Why do you always say Finland?"

"I don't always say Finland. Why would I always

say Finland?"

"I don't know. You just do."

"I don't."

"You do."

"I most certainly do not," the local exclaimed and tried to look offended but due to bad acting skills he just looked silly. "Just five minutes ago I said Greece. I don't always say Finland."

"When I say always, I don't mean always as in always," said the blond and hesitated for a while as if to think whether what he had just said had really been what he had meant to say. "I mean, you always say Finland this and Finland that when you refer to my home country."

"I don't."

"You do."

"I do?"

"You do."

"Do I?" asked the local looking genuinely surprised. No acting skills were needed this time. "Did I say Finland just now?"

"You said Finland just now," replied the blond and sighed. "And yesterday. And last week. And the week before that."

"And the week before that?"

"And the week before that!"

"I don't remember." The local looked unconvinced about the wild accusations made by the blond. "Did I really say Finland?"

"Yes, you really said Finland," replied the blond trying to sound slightly annoyed like some people get when answering repeatedly silly questions asked by children. Like the local, the blond wasn't a good actor either. "But you are not the only one. For some reason, many people mistakenly call me Finnish even if they know very well that I am Icelandic. They also repeatedly talk about Finland this and Finland that. It is weird."

"Weird indeed," the local replied and rubbed his chin as if he was thinking very hard about something.

The two men were silent for a moment and sipped their beer. Both of them looked as if they were thinking. The presumed local rubbing his chin, and the man who one would guess was either Swedish or Norwegian scratching his head. They both stared at their beer seemingly hoping the bubbles would bring some knowledge to the surface that could help them shed light on the weird situation.

The square was quiet again. The drivers had stopped honking their horns long ago. The driver and the passer-by had said their goodbyes and the traffic was not blocked anymore.

"Are you sure it isn't you?" the one that one would guess was a local asked suddenly.

"Me?" the blond replied and raised his eyebrows as if he wanted to underline his incomprehension of the question. Again their acting skills let the men down.

"Yes," replied the local. "Since going on about Finland this and Finland that is not really restricted to me, but is a general trend, have you ever wondered whether it could be you?"

"You mean that I hear Finland instead of Iceland?"

"Well, yes. That could be it ..." the local paused a bit before continuing. He did not look entirely convinced whether he should continue at all. "Or it could be that you are really Finnish."

"No, wait. I'm pretty sure I'm not Finnish."

There was another moment of silence that both men used to sip their beer in the hope they could consume some of the knowledge the bubbles might have brought to the surface.

"Ever heard about the wisdom of crowds?" the local asked.

"No."

"The basic idea is that often an uninformed crowd

26

can collectively be wiser than a single expert."

"So, ..." the blond hesitated for a while as if to comprehend the wisdom put forward by the local. "You are saying that since a crowd frequently refers to me as Finnish, I should question my own expertise in determining my own nationality?"

"It is just a theory," the local said shrugging his shoulders.

"I don't think so," said the blond shaking his head.

"Well. You are probably right," admitted the local with a frown – which turned quickly back into a smile as if he had been struck by a brilliant idea. "Maybe it is probability."

"Probability?" the blond looked puzzled.

"Yes," replied the local and looked excited about elaborating on his idea. "People know that you are Nordic but not Scandinavian – in the Scandinavian Airlines sense of Scandinavian. If you put all non-Scandinavian Nordic people into a hat and draw one at random then you are much more likely to draw a Finn than an Icelandic person. Therefore, many people accidentally refer to you as Finnish. They can't help it. It is just the law of probabilities."

The man who one would have guessed was either Swedish or Norwegian shook his head in disbelief and stared at the local. The local stared back.

"How long have we known each other?" asked the blond.

"Six months," answered the local, and now it was his turn to look puzzled. "Why?"

"We have known each other for six months and yet you still consider me to be just some random non-Scandinavian Nordic person drawn from a hat?"

"Well, I didn't mean it like that," the local replied, and his uniform tan went slightly red. He looked embarrassed. "You know what I meant."

"Ja, ja," admitted the blond with an accent that one would only associate with someone from either Sweden or Norway. He smiled and seemed to know exactly what the local meant.

"Anyways, what is your answer?" asked the local.

"What was the question?" asked the blond who had apparently forgotten the question that had originated the whole discussion.

"What is the traffic like in Finland?"

RAIN IN KRAKÓW

I shook the raindrops off my coat before taking a seat next to the window of a nearly empty café. My plans had changed. After a week-long meeting I longed for fresh air. I had planned to use the weekend to wander about in Kraków. Get to know the city. Take some photos. The skies had other ideas, though. The weather was not on my side.

"Co dla Pana?"

I looked at the waitress who had addressed me. I guessed that she was asking if I wanted anything. What she could get me, or something like that.

"Sorry, I don't speak Polish," I replied.

"Oh, I was just asking if I could get you something," she replied in English. "I thought you were Polish. You have a Polish aura."

I ordered a latte and a croissant. I looked across the square. The rain was pouring down. There were few people out in the rain and I was the only customer in the café. I dug my notebook and a pen out of my backpack. I wanted to write a description in the atmosphere on the square. Kill time. Perhaps I could write it into a short story.

"Where are you from?" the waitress asked as she brought me my coffee and croissant.

"Iceland," I replied. "Reykjavík."

"Oh, Iceland," she said in a dreamy voice looking out of the window and across the square. "I have heard it is beautiful. And many Polish people have gone there to work."

The waitress left me with my coffee and returned to the bar. I took a bite of the croissant and sipped the coffee. I looked around me, across the square and around the mostly empty café, in search of inspiration for my writing.

Loud music played in the café – mixed with the conversations of the two waitresses who were both talking on their phones. I did not understand what they said, but could imagine that their conversations were quite different. I guessed that the one who had served me was having an argument with her mother while the other was speaking to her boyfriend. One was shouting but the other spoke softly, blushing from time to time and laughing timidly.

"I have told you many times that I am not coming back," the angry sounding waitress shouted at the phone and hung up. She was tired of how her mother insisted she return to the village. She was not going back home. She had made up her mind. She was going to stay here in Kraków and earn money for her trip around the world. Her mother was still hoping she would return to the village and marry the priest's son. She, however, had made up her mind. She would not marry him. Their relationship was over. They did not have anything in common anymore.

They had been close in their youth – she and the priest's son. They had played together. They had daydreamed together. They had decided to travel the world together. They had spent hours upon hours dreaming of faraway cities in faraway continents. The world was theirs and they were going to explore it. Their dreams started with the big Polish cities – Warsaw and Kraków. They would often lie in the fields outside their village and make up stories about their future lives in the cities. Later, they dreamt of big European cities – London, Berlin and Paris. They spent many hours in the school library studying books about foreign places. Gradually, their dreams moved on to even more faraway places – America and Asia. Their dreams had no borders.

As they grew older they started to grow apart. She continued dreaming of faraway places, while his thoughts moved closer to home. He decided to follow in his father's footsteps and take over the priesthood of the village. The world stopped calling him. The priesthood became his calling. He stopped dreaming of the world. His world consisted of the people in the village and their relationship with God. He had tried to convince her to stay by his side as the priest's wife, but he had given up after a while when he realized that he was far from convincing her.

I stopped writing, asking myself whether catholic priests could get married at all. Something told me they could not. I wrote a note to myself reminding me to look it up when I got home. I was not sure if I was going anywhere with this story. I put the lid on the pen and looked across the square. It was still raining heavily. Few customers had shown up at the market to buy food for supper. The street vendors stood under their tents discussing the weather. Or, at least, I presumed they were discussing the weather. It did not seem likely that the rain would stop any time soon. There was thus nothing for me to do than return to writing my story. I looked to the bar. Now there was only one waitress there. The one who had served me. The one who had been speaking angrily on the phone. There were no other customers. She killed time by polishing the bar.

The night before her eighteenth birthday she had packed her most essential things. Before dawn the following day she snuck out of the house without being noticed. She left a letter for her parents. She told them she had gone to see the world. She told them not to worry about her. She was a grown-up now and could take care of herself. She told them she would call.

She arrived in Kraków shortly before noon. She started walking from one restaurant to another looking for a job. She had heard that restaurants and cafés were the best places to seek work. The job hunt was not as easy as she had imagined in her daydreams. Nobody wanted to hire an inexperienced girl from the countryside. She had been hopeful when she left her village in the early morning, but as the evening drew closer she conceded that finding a job would take some time. However, she did not give up all hope. She was sure she could handle it. She had saved enough money to stay a few nights at the cheapest guesthouse in town. Those few nights would give her time to find work. Some job. Any job.

The following day she continued her job hunt. She gave up on the restaurants and turned her attention to the bars and cafés. She kept her standards high to begin with and explored the posh cafés. Gradually she let her standards drop and went for the less posh cafés. By the end of the day she had managed to get a job as a dishwasher and waitress at a bar downtown. The working hours were long. The pay was poor. She barely managed to make a living. She stole old bread and other leftovers that were put aside at the end of the day.

And so the first few weeks went by in the world outside her village. Life was far from being anything close to what she had imagined in her daydreams. However, she kept her hopes high. She thought that this was only the beginning. Things would get better as time went by.

Now a year had passed since she had moved to the city and she was celebrating her nineteenth birthday in solitude. She had long ago lost count of the bars and cafés she had worked in. She had gradually managed to work her way up the gastronomic ladder. She was far from her dream of exploring the world. Nevertheless, she had not given up hope. She kept her dream alive. She was going to go to Berlin, London or Paris as soon as she could.

She called home once a week to let her parents know that she was fine. She was careful not to let them know where she was or what she did for a living. She wanted to keep them at a certain distance. Every phone call ended with an argument with her mother who wanted her to return to the village. She remained loyal to her dream. She was not going to go back. She was going to explore the world. And so ended today's phone call, like all the others.

She sat behind the bar and looked across the square. The rain was pouring down. The café was almost empty. A foreigner with glasses, sideburns and goatee sat by one window. He was writing furiously. Occasionally he looked up from his notebook, letting his eyes wander across the square and taking a sip of his coffee before continuing his writing. When he had entered the café she had thought he was Polish, but he had not understood anything when she had asked him what she could get him. When she had asked him where he was from, he had said he was from Iceland. She found it curious. During all her daydreaming her mind had never travelled to Iceland. She had heard of some Polish people who had found work on that mysterious remote island. But Reykjavík did not sound as attractive as Berlin, London or Paris. However, she thought she should not exclude it as an option. She wondered if she should ask him for his card in case he could help her find a job in Reykjavík.

"You have changed!"

She looked at the customer who had entered the café without her noticing him. She could hardly believe her eyes. He had also changed. He had a beard and wore glasses. He looked older. He had grown up – somewhat. He looked more like a priest than the son of a priest.

"So have you," she answered timidly, feeling herself blushing.

They smiled awkwardly at each other. They were shy. They, who had played together every day when they were younger. They, who had known each other better than they had known anybody else.

"I am going to Paris," he said, pushing his glasses higher up his nose.

She stared at him not knowing whether to laugh or cry. For so long she had dreamt of hearing those words. In another context though. She had dreamt they were going to Paris together.

"I want you to come with me," he continued, smiling awkwardly.

She did not know what to say. Too long time had passed since they had lain together in the grass outside their village and dreamt about going to Paris together.

"I am going to a seminary in Paris. I want you to come with me. I have a small apartment arranged by the school."

She smiled. He had aged and matured, but deep inside he was still an innocent boy from the countryside.

"And what do you think the teachers at the seminary will say when you bring a girl with you to Paris? You, the unmarried priest pupil?"

He did not answer right away. He looked puzzled. He had apparently not thought this through. He looked away and stared at the bottles behind the bar. As if he could find the answer in a bottle. She shook her head. She waited for him to answer. She polished the bar.

They remained silent.

"I will tell them you are my sister. I will tell them that you are with me to help me while I study. To do the laundry, cook and that sort of things."

He looked at her again. So innocent. So sure of himself.

"It will not work. It is better if you go alone."

She felt a lump in her throat as she said this. She looked away, secretly wiping away a tear that had formed in her eye. She could not go with him. Not under these circumstances.

"Ok, well, if you change your mind, here is my address in Paris. I will take the train tomorrow morning."

He gave her a card with a trembling hand.

"I might write you a postcard," she said, forcing a sympathetic smile.

She said this to justify accepting his card. She did not want him to think that she was considering going after him. She did not want to raise false expectations.

He said goodbye and left. As soon as he was gone she was overcome by emotions. Tears rolled down her cheeks. She could not hold them back. She thought about the times when they had dreamt about exploring the world together. That dream had never been as close to becoming reality as now. Yet it seemed so far away. She wished it could come true but deep inside she knew it would not. They had grown apart. He was still a boy from the village. She was now a woman in the city. They were too different.

I looked up from my notebook, looked out the window and across the square. The rain had stopped. It was time to put my previous plans into action. It was time to wander about in the city. This short story could wait until later. Moreover, I was not sure if it was on its way to becoming something or not. I didn't know enough about the life of young catholic priests in Polish villages. It would be difficult for me to make this story realistic. I packed my notebook into my backpack and went to the bar to pay my bill. It was time to explore Kraków.

"Here is my card," I said as I paid my bill. "You can contact me if you decide to try your luck and find a job in Reykjavík."

I had surprised myself by giving the waitress my business card. The act was spontaneous and without much thought. I did not know why I had done it. Maybe I was having trouble distinguishing between reality and the fiction I had been writing.

She watched the customer leave the café and walk into the square. It had stopped raining. She looked at the card. She wondered if she should accept the offer. Was this at last her chance to go and explore the big wide world? At worst, she could live with him for a few days while she looked for a job and found her own place. She put the card in her pocket. She would sleep on it and decide later.

WHAT DO FISH EAT?

"What do fish eat?"

I turned around in my chair and looked in the direction of my office door where my colleague was staring at me with questioning eyes. His question came as a complete surprise to me. I did not know how to react. What do fish eat? Was this some sort of riddle? Was it a play of words? Was it a general question about the diet of marine species? The question sounded simple, but I had no idea what it meant. I could not imagine what could have prompted it. My guess was that it was some sort of strange joke.

"You are from Iceland, right?" my colleague asked after having given up on waiting for an answer to his original question.

"Yes," I replied hesitantly, unable to comprehend how that fact had anything to do with the original question. I put my joke theory aside, unless my nationality had something to do with the pun.

"Then you must know something about the diet of fish," my colleague claimed. By now I was certain that this was not a joke, my colleague looked too serious.

"Well, I guess it depends on the type of fish," I answered rather unconvincingly. "I guess that some eat plankton and others maybe eat shrimp. I must however admit that I know very little about the diet of fish. My priority is for fish to be part of my diet rather than bothering about what they themselves eat."

My lack of knowledge on the subject was no understatement. If I had ever learned about it in biology class, I had certainly forgotten all about it by now. I was also surprised about being asked this question by my colleague. We were both PhD students in rather non-biological subjects – I in computer science and he in mathematical logic. The subject of the diet of fish was not really a common one in our part of the university.

"But fish in tanks?" my colleague continued. "Goldfish. What do they eat?"

"Fish food," I guessed. "I guess."

I was surprised how unconvincing my answer sounded. In particular in the light of how obvious it was. The logician should not need the help of a computer scientist to reach that conclusion. I wondered again whether it was some sort of logical trick question. Maybe a non-obvious question that asked for a non-obvious answer.

"That's what I thought as well," my colleague answered, nodding his head.

We remained silent for a while. My colleague stared out of the window, looking as if he was thinking very deeply about something. This was obviously no logical trick question, my colleague looked too serious. I was curious to know what this was all about, since the whole situation was rather absurd.

"Why do you ask?" I asked my colleague to try to satisfy my curiosity.

"My flatmate has gone on a trip for a few days and she left me a note to remind me to feed the fish," my colleague replied. "However, she said nothing about what I should feed them, when, or how much. I am a bit puzzled. I don't know what to do."

My colleague did indeed look puzzled and a little helpless.

"Are you sure that there is no fish food in the vicinity of the tank?" I asked, rather skeptical that my colleague's assignment was as complex as he seemed to think.

"I looked for some, but found nothing," my colleague admitted and sighed. "What does fish food look like, anyway?"

As I had never kept fish myself I had limited knowledge of fish food. I recalled a moment from my childhood, seeing a friend of mine mince some sort of mixture of green leaves for his fish. That was all I knew about keeping fish.

"As far as I know, fish food is some sort of minced leaves in a small cylindrical container," I suggested trying not to sound more knowledgeable than I really was.

"That's what I thought as well," my colleague replied. "But I could see no such thing anywhere close to the fish tank."

It struck me how hopeless my colleague looked when confronted with this problem. I knew him as the authentic genius who could find a solution to any question that came up in the field of mathematical logic. However, to this elementary problem of pet keeping, he could not find an answer. I decided to help him by continuing to point out the obvious.

"Why don't you go to a pet shop and ask for fish food?" I suggested and felt the same embarrassing sensation of silliness I always got when I answered an obvious question put forward by a professor in the classroom.

"That's a good point," my colleague replied and seemed relieved for a while before returning to his previous hopelessness. "Where do I find a pet shop?"

I thought about it for a while but I could not remember ever having passed a pet shop in the three years I had lived in Amsterdam. In my defense, I had never needed anything from a pet shop, so I guessed it was normal that I had not noticed any – even if I had passed one.

"No clue. I do not recall having seen such a shop," I admitted. "As I said before, I have very limited knowledge of these fishy matters. When it comes to me and fish food, it is the fish that is the food and I am the one who is doing the eating."

"So, I guess the logical conclusion to all of this would be that if I should try to make use of your experience in these matters, it would make sense for me to eat the fish," the colleague deduced, smiling. He was apparently not too worried about not having found a sensible solution to his problem.

"You are the logician," I replied. "I will not argue against your reasoning in this case. However, you might want to google a pet shop before you prepare dinner."

"Thanks! I'll figure something out," my colleague said as he left my office. "In the worst case scenario I could find a good goldfish recipe."

I could not but wonder if he was going to have fish for dinner.

★ ★ ★ ★ ★

"Ta-da! Guess what this is?"

I turned around in my chair and looked in the direction of my office door where my colleague stood smiling with a small cylindrical container in his hand, which to me looked likely to contain dried parsley.

"Dried parsley?" I replied.

"Fish food?" my colleague asked as he handed me the cylindrical container.

"No, dried parsley," I reiterated.

"Are you sure it is not fish food?" my colleague asked, the smile disappearing from his lips.

"Yes, I am very sure. This is a spice used to flavor fish before putting it in the oven, not something used to feed it."

"But say someone fed this to fish, would it hurt them?"

Again, I did not have the right experience to answer my colleague's question. In fact, I did indeed doubt that anyone had the right experience to answer that question. Yet.

"I'm not sure," I replied. "I know however that parsley is ideal if you want to cook fish in the oven. Did you feed parsley to the fish?"

"Err, yes," my colleague replied awkwardly.

"Why?"

I almost could not resist laughing at my colleague's misfortune. I tried to hold it back though, since my colleague did not seem to share my joyfulness.

"I went home with your description of fish food in mind. I looked around the house for a container full of minced dried leaves. This was the only thing that matched that definition."

"Did you find the parsley close to the fish tank?"

"Well, not that close to the fish tank, it was in a

47

cupboard in the kitchen."

"Maybe between the salt and pepper?" I asked unable to hold back a nasty grin.

"Well, perhaps not between them," my colleague replied. "But in the same general area. Well, the same shelf."

"It did not occur to you that since the container was on the same shelf as the salt and pepper that it might be some sort of spice used for cooking?"

"No, not really. That did not occur to me. I guess I was so determined to find fish food that I did not think about that."

"So, you gave the fish parsley?"

"Yes," my colleague replied, looking rather awkward. He seemed to be realizing the mistake he had made.

"Did they eat the parsley?"

"Like candy," my colleague replied, smiling as if he was recalling some good old memory from the past.

"And they are still alive?"

"Well, they were alive when I left for the office this morning."

"Not floating on their back close to the surface?"

"Not floating on their back close to the surface."

"Interesting!" I said. "Maybe parsley is a decent

food for fish after all. However, if I were you, I would still google a pet shop. Just in case long term parsley consumption does have some unexpected side effects for goldfish."

"I will. Thanks for the advice," my colleague replied as he left my office with the parsley in one hand and a smile on his face.

★ ★ ★ ★ ★

"Is it normal that fish change color?"

I turned around in my chair and looked in the direction of my office door where my colleague was standing for the third consecutive day asking a fish related question. Although I was getting used to weird questions, this one was the weirdest one so far.

"Pardon?" I asked to make sure I had heard correctly.

"Is it normal that fish change color?"

I had probably heard correctly. At least I had heard the same thing twice in a row. I thought of the parsley, and of lollipop-green goldfish swimming in a tank.

"Well, I think that some marine animals can change colors in order to assimilate their surroundings and thereby avoid being eaten by other marine animals," I answered even though I was sure that my colleague's question was not about the general adaptability of marine life.

"I mean goldfish. Is it normal that they change color. From yellow-ish to green-ish?"

"Green-ish goldfish, you say. Have the parsley eating goldfish changed colors?" I asked, trying to hold back the laughter that was boiling inside me. "Have they turned green?"

"Err, yes," my colleague answered nervously.

"But they are alive?"

"Yes, alive. But green."

Once again I had to admit that my colleague's problem was far beyond my core competence.

"I must admit that I have limited experience of the effect of feeding parsley to goldfish. I cannot say if this color change is a normal reaction or not," I said with as straight a face as I could maintain. "I can however confirm that oven baked fish with parsley does not change colors. Or at least it does not turn green."

"Oh well," was all my colleague had to say before going back to his office.

* * * * *

"Do you have Sipser?"

I turned around in my chair and looked in the direction of my office door where my colleague had once again appeared with a question on his lips. It took me a while to digest the question. The question was abnormally normal. The question was somewhat understandable, did not involve color-changing, parsley-eating goldfish and made sense in the context of an office space inhabited largely by mathematicians, logicians and theoretical computer scientists.

"You mean 'Introduction to the Theory of Computation'?" I asked just to be sure I had heard correctly, and was not missing some hidden connection to either the diet or metamorphosis of goldfish.

"Yes," my colleague confirmed. "I need to look up a definition."

I handed him the book and told him he could take it with him and return it when he was done. He thanked me and prepared to return to his own office.

"By the way, how did it go with the goldfish?" I asked before he could leave the office. "Did they survive the parsley?"

"Err, well, yes," my colleague answered awkwardly. "They remained green for a week. My flatmate got a shock when she returned. She thought I had killed the fish and replaced them with green ones."

"But they recovered?"

"Yes. They are now back to their golden yellow color."

"Did you ask her about the fish food?"

"Well, yes," my colleague answered and blushed slightly but did not seem to have any intention of elaborating on that answer.

"And?" I asked to try to drag the story out of him.

"Well, the thing is that the box with the fish food was on top of the note that she left me. I thought it was some sort of spice so I put it in the fridge."

"The fridge?"

"Well, yes," my colleague replied and paused before continuing. "How is it going with the upper bound of that algorithm you were studying last week, by the way?"

I smiled. My colleague had apparently had enough of fish related discussion for the time being.

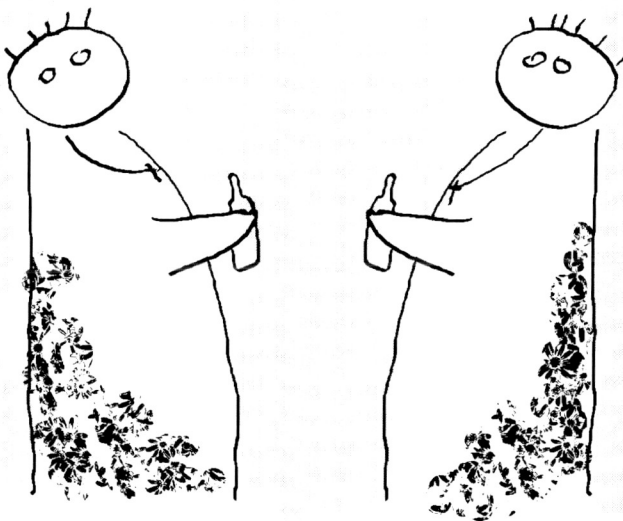

THE NEIGHBORS

"Welcome to my new palace," I said to Katrín as she entered the apartment I had moved into a few days earlier.

"Thank you, your highness," she replied, winking and bowing.

I grinned. That's what I liked about Katrín. She never took life too seriously. Yet she was also someone with whom you could talk about serious things when you needed to. In my years abroad I had never made an effort to be around my Icelandic compatriots. It was not that I disliked them. In my view there were just so many amusing foreigners here abroad that I did not have any special need to fish in Icelandic waters. Katrín was however genuinely amusing and I would make an effort to maintain our friendship.

"The bedroom, the bathroom, the kitchen, the storage room, the living room and the dining room."

I introduced her to my new apartment as we made our way from the front door to the dining room.

"Wow, a dining room," Katrín said with a mocking look on her face. "How impressive. Just like a proper palace."

"Indeed. Except in proper palaces the dining table normally seats more than four people."

I looked at my small Ikea dining table. Although technically one could fit four people around it, in practice one could only comfortably fit two. The dining room did however not accommodate a larger table.

"Well, you cannot have it all. At least you have a dining room. Not all inhabitants of Barcelona can afford to waste a whole room for a dining table."

"I would not call it a waste," I said trying to look profound. "I would call it an investment."

"Why?" Katrín asked.

"I don't really know," I answered, feeling a bit embarrassed.

I really did not know. It was just one of those silly spontaneous statements I made every now and then because I thought they sounded funny. I had not really thought about what it meant. Let alone whether it was at all funny.

"What is the neighborhood like?" Katrín asked.

"Splendid. I am in the center of Gràcia. A few steps away from Virreina square. What more can one ask for?"

"Is it not noisy?"

"No, the noise from Virreina square is absorbed by the church that is between me and the square. So it is actually rather quiet."

"The silencing effect of the catholic church has always been strong," Katrín said and grinned. "And the neighbors? No noise from them?"

"None at all. Not any more than in any other old building in Barcelona," I said, trying to remember if I had ever noticed any abnormal noise from my neighbors. "Furthermore, across the street there is an abbey of monks. They are not really the noisy type."

"Monks?" Katrín asked with a hint of disbelief in

her voice.

"Yes, monks," I replied, sounding a bit insecure since the idea of living next door to an abbey of monks had not fully sunk in to my mind and was still fairly alien.

"Interesting," Katrín said. "They do have a nice terrace for barbecues, though. It would be a pity if they do not use it."

There was a short silence. She was right. I looked over to the terrace of the abbey. It would be a pity if they did not use it. My mind started to imagine what it would look like with a group of monks throwing a barbecue party. In my mind it looked surreal. As I could not recall ever having seen monks in real life I imagined a group of bald men in heavy brown cloaks, drinking beer from one-liter bottles and barbecuing juicy burgers. The vision was based on an episode from The Simpsons, mixed with scenes from The Name of the Rose. It was accordingly surrealistic.

"Coffee?" I asked, trying to get the bald, beer-drinking, barbecuing monks out of my mind.

"Sure," Katrín replied and made herself comfortable on the sofa.

I went into the kitchen and started preparing the coffee. I could hear Katrín get off the sofa and walk across the living room. I guessed she was taking another look at the view of my neighborhood.

"Do monks in Spain normally wear women's clothing?" I heard Katrín shout from the living room.

"Sorry?" I shouted back since I was not sure if I had heard her correctly.

"Do monks in Spain normally wear women's clothing?"

I guessed I had heard her correctly the first time. I was not sure if I understood where she was going with her question but I most likely had heard her correctly.

"I would not know," I said as I handed her a cup of coffee and joined her at the living room window overlooking the terrace of the abbey. "I don't think I have ever seen Spanish monks. I haven't even seen my neighbors."

We sipped our coffee, admiring the view. The monks' terrace was partially covered by a roof made of semi-transparent plastic. In the roof-covered part of the terrace, the abbey's inhabitants were hanging out laundry.

"You can see why I asked you that question." Katrín said.

"Yes, I see."

I could see why she had asked me that question. From under the roof of the terrace I could see the bottom third of my neighbors' bodies. I could see their brown slippers, their bare ankles and the lower part of their calves, the bottom part of their dark blue skirts and their light blue aprons. The outfit was rather different from the heavy brown cloaks I had imagined some minutes before.

"Those monks of yours seem to be in good touch with their feminine side," Katrín said after we had stood in silence for a while admiring the bottom third of my new neighbors. "Maybe they belong to some sort of cult of cross-dressing monks. Strange. For monks at least."

"Who are we to judge them?" I asked. "They report to God, but not to the superficial fashion norms set by our modern society. If they want to wear women's clothing it is between them and God. If God approves, they can wear whatever they want to wear. Be it heavy brown cloaks, be it jeans or be it skirts and aprons."

"You are right," Katrín said and put on a serious face. "We should not be blinded by our backward views of gender stereotypes. If those monks want to wear skirts, it is none but their own business."

We looked at each other and smiled. Content with our intelligent sounding slogans of modern moral views, we moved away from the window and made ourselves comfortable on the sofa.

"Out of curiosity," Katrín continued after we had sat in silence for a while enjoying our coffee. "Since you had never seen your neighbors before, how did you know they were monks?"

"The landlord told me."

"What did he say exactly?"

"I don't remember exactly what she said," I replied, trying to remember what the landlord had said exactly. "It sounded something like monk at least."

We sat in silence for a while. Katrín looked as if there were some elaborate thoughts forming in her mind.

"Do you have a Spanish dictionary?" she asked.

"Yes, of course," I replied and went to fetch my Spanish-English / English-Spanish dictionary from the bookshelf. "What's on your mind?"

"Do you know how you say nun in Spanish?" Katrín asked as she browsed the dictionary.

"Well, no," I replied and grinned. "For some reason that word has not entered my vocabulary of everyday Spanish."

Katrín stopped her browsing and pointed her index finger at a page in the latter half of the dictionary.

"Well, according to this dictionary of yours, the

word for nun is 'monja' in Spanish."

That was an interesting observation. In retrospect it was not all that surprising. It might well explain some things.

"So, if I understand you correctly, you are implying that maybe my neighbors might be nuns rather than a cult of cross-dressing monks?"

"Well, I hate to destroy your fantasy of living next door to a cult of cross-dressing monks," Katrín said with a grin, "but it is plausible that your neighbors are indeed nuns."

"Hmm. Either way. Getting back to the original point, I do not expect the quietness of my new apartment to be disturbed by any wild parties coming from across the street."

THE DARKNESS

"Did you know that things exist that one sees better in darkness than in daylight?" you asked as we walked together in the darkness along the unlit gravel road that ran the length of the fjord in western Iceland.

"No," I replied. "Like what?"

"Like ghosts, demons, gnomes, elves, and things like that," you continued. "Anything that cannot tolerate the light of day."

"But ghosts do not exist in reality," I claimed, although against my own conviction. I bit my lower lip and felt a shiver run down my spine.

You did not reply but giggled.

We had been at a bonfire party but were now on our way to the farmhouse we used as our vacation home. Mom and dad had decided to stay longer at the party and have fun with the other adults. Mom had asked you to take me home. You were three years older than I, and it was thus your responsibility to bring the two of us home.

The night was pitch-black. Behind us was a faint glow of the cooling bonfire. On the other side of the fjord we could see the lights of distant farms. The lights of the farms on our side of the fjord were hidden beyond the dense birch woods that separated the farms and the road. We could see neither the moon nor the stars since the sky was completely covered by clouds. We could not see where we were going and had to put all our faith in the fact that we had walked this road so often before that we could find our way blindfolded. And so we did, quite literally, blindfolded by the darkness.

The night was silent. We were silent. We heard little other than the crunch of gravel from under our feet as we walked. Occasionally we could hear a faint sound of laughter coming from the party. Otherwise, it was completely silent. Completely silent and completely dark.

All of a sudden an opening appeared in the cloud cover. The curtains of the sky opened and nature put on a show for us. The moon stepped onto the the stage and lit up our surroundings. Shadows ran along the road. A gust of wind blew down along the fjord. The birch trees waved their branches back and forth.

The show ended as suddenly as it had started. The opening in the cloud cover closed. The curtains of the sky closed. The darkness returned.

"Did you see that?" you asked as you grabbed my arm and forced me to stop.

"No," I lied, because I was not sure what it was that I had seen. I had seen something. Something that had been creeping by the road. Something that had moved as the moon had broken its way through the clouds. Something that swayed in time with the birch branches.

"Neither did I," you said and giggled.

I felt a shiver run through my body. A lump formed in my stomach. I knew you were playing with me. I knew you were trying to intensify my fear of the dark.

I did not want the fright to take control of my mind. I wanted to forget what I had seen. I wanted to have seen nothing. But since you had mentioned it, I could not help wondering whether I had really seen something. Something that maybe could not bear the light of day.

We remained silent during the remainder of the walk home. I listened to every crunch from beneath our feet. Was it really from beneath our feet? Or was it maybe from behind us? Or maybe ahead of us? I could not tell. As I could not see anything, I gave my imagination full freedom to fill in the gaps. I listened to every sound that came from the birch woods. Was there something out there? I could feel my heart beating faster. Was it really only my heartbeat that I was feeling? The fright had really taken control of my body.

I felt a great sense of relief when we reached the farmhouse and were able to turn on the lights. At last we could see our surroundings – our immediate surroundings at least. I felt better – slightly calmer. Yet I still had not fully recovered from the walk through the darkness. I could not stop thinking about what I had seen during that short period of moonlight. I could not stop thinking about your words about seeing things that could not tolerate daylight. I could not avoid the echo of your creepy giggle in my head. I could not stop wondering whether there really had been something out there.

"Good night," you said with a grin on your face when we had brushed our teeth and prepared for bed. "Sweet dreams."

You giggled as you walked over to your room. You knew that my dreams would not be sweet. You knew that you had intensified the fear inside me. You knew about my fear of the dark.

I twisted and turned in my bed and I could not sleep. I listened to every sound coming out of the darkness. I listened to the creaks from the wooden beams of the roof. I listened to the sound of birch branches scraping against the walls of the house.

I knew that ghosts did not exist. Or so I told myself. However, I could not avoid imagining someone running along the rooftop whenever I heard the creak of a roof beam. Whenever I heard the scraping of the birch branches I could not avoid the image of a phantom running along the walls of the house, peeking into every window. You had succeeded in scaring me. I could feel the presence of something outside. It crept in. I could feel the presence of something in my room. I kept completely still under my bed covers, listening to my own heartbeat.

All of a sudden I heard a smack, followed by a low squeak. My heartbeat went up a notch. I took a deep breath and tried to control myself. I managed to calm myself slightly. I rose quietly and got out of bed. I walked slowly towards the door in search of the light switch. I turned on the light.

My eyes wandered around the bedroom. In a corner I could see what had caused the smack and the squeak. A mouse had been caught in a trap.

I bent down and studied the mouse. It looked at me with praying eyes. I smiled. I would set it free. It need not worry. It was beneficial for the both of us. I put my hand gently around the body of the mouse and released it from the mousetrap. I straightened up and stroked the mouse. I could feel its heart beating fast. It was frightened. As frightened as I had been just minutes before.

I opened the door and walked into the darkness outside my bedroom. I tiptoed along the corridor toward your room. I opened the door and crept in. I could not see much in the dark but I could hear that you were fast asleep. I put the mouse carefully on the edge of your bed, tiptoed back to the corridor and closed the door as quietly as I could.

I had barely made it back to my bed when I heard you scream. I knew how much you hated mice. You were as afraid of mice as I was afraid of the darkness. We were equal now. My heartbeat slowed down. I stopped listening to the creaks from the roof beams. I stopped listening to the scraping of the branches. I fell asleep. I dreamt of mice.

JULIA

I drove the Ferrari down my throat. A chill went through my body. I coughed. This had to be it. I could not take any more shots. I stumbled along the bar of this fairly typical Irish pub in the gothic quarter of Barcelona. A narrow but long space. At the front, close to the entrance, was the bar. At the back of the pub was a space with tables and chairs. I stumbled towards the back where the lights had been turned off and the chairs had been put on top of the tables in order to facilitate the cleaning that would be done after the pub closed. I was still coughing. This would be my last Ferrari. My last shot. Vodka and Tia Maria was not the right mixture for me. I was switching to vodka tonic.

"Are you all right?"

I peered into the darkness to try to see where the words had come from. At first I saw nothing. Nothing but darkness. When I peered more closely into the dark empty space I saw her sitting at a table. Alone in the dark sipping a Coronita.

"My name's Julia," she said with an accent that reminded me of English movies from the 1930s. I was not sure if I had ever seen any English movies from the 1930s, but that was what came to my mind. She was like that girl in Pygmalion. Or was it Mary Poppins? She was English. Right? Mary Poppins, that is. I didn't know. I could not think clearly. I was too drunk.

"Hey Julie, I'm Vilhelm." I said. "Why are you sitting here alone in the dark?"

"I don't know," she replied. "And my name is Julia. Why don't you sit down here next to me? That way I would not be alone anymore."

I hesitated. She had caught me off guard. I did

not know if I should stay or go. There was something special about this girl. She looked so innocent. Almost like an angel. Well, apart from the Coronita. I did not think I had ever before seen an angel with a bottle of beer in their hand. Come to think of it, I had never actually seen an angel, with or without a Coronita in their hand. I was confused. I was not thinking straight. I had had too many shots.

"Why don't you join us?" I asked finally and pointed in the direction of my friends who were at the bar. "My friends are over there."

"I don't know if I should," she said and looked down at her bottle as if she was reading the answer from the label. "Well, yes, maybe I will."

She stood up and we walked towards the bar where my friends were ordering another round of Ferraris.

"Where are you from?" I asked her.

"Austria," she replied. "And you?"

"Iceland," I said as I leaned against the bar and tried to get my friends attention. "Guys, listen. This is Julie. From Austria."

It took my friends a few moments to notice my introduction. They were too busy taking delivery of their order of vodka and Tia Maria shots.

"Who?" Patrick asked when the shots were on the

table.

"Her," I said and turned to look at Julie. She was gone. Behind me was nothing but a half-full bottle of Coronita sitting on the bar.

"Who?" Danny asked.

"I don't know," I replied as I accepted the shot of Ferrari that Patrick was handing me.

"To Vilhelm and all his imaginary friends!" Danny proposed and we downed the Ferrari.

I coughed again and my mind replayed what had happened in the past few minutes. I thought of Julie. Was she really a figment of my imagination? Probably, I admitted. I was pretty drunk. But what about that half-full Coronita bottle? I touched it. The bottle was clearly not imaginary. I was confused. I ordered a vodka tonic.

★ ★ ★ ★ ★

I leaned my head against the window of the subway car. I closed my eyes. It was supposed to have merely been a simple business dinner with a client. I had promised myself that I wouldn't continue drinking afterwards. I had not kept my promise. This was happening too often. As an accountant my whole existence was about keeping the books balanced. Why then could I not keep my life in the same balance?

The train pulled into Joanic station. It was time for me to get off and head home to bed. I stood up and walked towards the door. As I got out of the car I met the eyes of a young woman getting in.

"Julie?" I asked as I turned around on the platform.

"Julia," she answered as the doors of the car closed.

We held eye-contact while the train made its way out of the station. Then she was gone. She had disappeared into the darkness. Just as she had done at the Irish pub a couple of days earlier. Was it my imagination? I could not tell. It felt so real. Yet so surreal.

★ ★ ★ ★ ★

I wandered along the empty street, through the dense fog. I did not know where I was. I did not know the street I was on. There was nobody around. Well, almost nobody. Someone was walking towards me, reciting a verse.

Byrði betri
ber-at maður brautu að
en sé mannvit mikið.
Vegnest verra

73

vegur-a hann velli að
en sé ofdrykkja öls.

I recognized the poem. It was one of the old Icelandic poems. If I recalled correctly it was called "Hávamál" and was a series of advices about how to live one's life.

Er-a svo gott
sem gott kveða
öl alda sonum,
því að færra veit
er fleira drekkur
síns til geðs gumi.

I could not see clearly the person reciting the poem. They were approaching me but I could only see their silhouette in the fog. The voice, however, was familiar. I had heard it sometime before.

Óminnishegri heitir
sá er yfir öldrum þrumir.
Hann stelur geði guma.
Þess fugls fjöðrum
eg fjötraður var'g
í garði Gunnlaðar.

Upon finishing the stanza the silhouette stepped out of the fog and I could see why I had recognized the voice. It was the young Austrian woman who I had met by coincidence a couple of times in the last few days. It was Julie. I wanted to ask her about the poem she had recited, but before I could speak, she transformed herself into a large bird and flew away.

★ ★ ★ ★ ★

I yawned before ringing the doorbell. I had not slept much after waking up from a strange dream about a young Austrian woman who had recited old Icelandic poetry before transforming herself into a bird.

I greeted my host and followed him from the front door into the living room. He introduced himself as Xavi. He was a friend of a friend. I had never met him before. My friend had told me that he and his wife were starting a company together and needed advice from an accountant. I had agreed to meet them over dinner and see if I could be of any help.

"Have a seat and make yourself comfortable," Xavi said, "I'll just check on the progress in the kitchen."

I looked around the living room. It was an interesting combination of modern and vintage design. In one corner a chest of drawers caught my attention. On top of it there was a large collection of framed photos. I walked over to take a closer look. In a handful of the photos I could recognize my host. The photos were Instagram vintage style photos in modern frames. Suddenly my gaze came to a halt and my eyes fixed on one of the photos. I picked it up in order to study it closer. It was also one of those vintage style photos. It was however not the style that caught my attention. It was the subject.

"Julie?" I said aloud to myself, trying to remember the name of the woman in the photo, the Austrian girl I had met twice by chance in the past few days, and once in my dreams.

"Julia," someone said from behind me, "Her name is Julia ... Well, yes, and welcome. I'm Núria."

My hostess had entered the room and was walking toward me smiling, but with a look of surprise on her face.

"How do you know Julia?" she asked as she looked over my shoulder to make sure that we were talking about the same photo.

"I don't really know her," I replied, "but I have met her by coincidence twice in the past few days."

Núria raised her eyebrows and looked at me with a look of disbelief in her eyes.

"That cannot be right," she said, "Julia died five years ago. She was my grandmother."

"Oh," I said, confused because I was sure that the woman in the photo was the same one I had met twice in the past few days. "I must have confused her with someone else."

"She was a good woman," Núria went on as I handed her the photo and she placed it back on the chest of drawers. "Born in Austria. She came to Spain with her parents when she was young. She married a Spanish factory owner, and spent most of her life helping factory workers overcome alcoholism."

I stared at the photo. My mind was in turmoil as it went over the events of the past few days.

"So, what can I get you?" Xavi asked as he entered the living room again. "Beer? Wine?"

I hesitated. Suddenly I did not feel like having anything alcoholic.

"Eh, I think a coke will be fine," I stuttered. "Or just water."

THE YOUNG MAN WITH THE
BICYCLE

I walked into the foyer carrying my bicycle down the hall. As I approached the door to my apartment I noticed a message had been slid between the door and the frame. I removed the folded paper and read the message written in neat handwriting.

"I've dropped some black underwear on to your patio. Regards, your neighbor in apartment 5-3."

I carried my bicycle to its place on the patio. On my way back into the apartment I picked up a black pair of women's underwear that lay on the floor of my patio. According to the note, it had fallen from my neighbor's clothesline – from the clothesline of apartment three on the fifth floor.

As I waited for the elevator to arrive it crossed my mind that this was the first time I had made use of it. In the year that had passed since I had moved to Barcelona I had never had any reason to visit my neighbors on the floors above me. In fact, come to think of it, I did not really know any of them. I recognized some by sight and greeted them if I met them in the foyer, but I knew none of them by name. I had given some of them descriptive names in my mind. There was the husband and wife who looked like brother and sister, the old man with the walking stick, the woman who always asked me if I had been away as she had not seen me in a while, the old couple with the grandchildren, etc. I felt a bit ashamed of only knowing them by their descriptions.

I left the elevator on the fifth floor and rang the doorbell at apartment 5-3. The door did not open but on the other side a dog barked enthusiastically. I wondered if it was trying to tell me to come back later. Perhaps it was telling me to stay away indefinitely. What did I know about dog language?

I was about to go back downstairs when the door of apartment 5-2 opened. An old woman with a wonky wig walked into the hallway, followed by a somewhat younger woman wearing a bathrobe. I had seen them both before but I had no descriptive names for them in my mind. Let alone real names.

"Hello young man!" said the old woman with the wonky wig and turned to the somewhat younger woman with the bathrobe. "It's the young man who dropped the bottle of red wine in the elevator."

"No," replied the somewhat younger woman with the bathrobe. "It is the young man with the bicycle."

"The young man with the bicycle?" The old woman with the wonky wig did not immediately grasp who was being referred to.

"Yes, the young man with the bicycle," repeated the somewhat younger woman with the bathrobe. "The young man on the ground floor. The foreigner with the goatee."

"Oh, yes. The young man with the bicycle!" The old woman with the wonky wig had seen the light. "I thought it was the young man who had dropped the

81

bottle of red wine in the elevator. I can see it now. It is the young man with the bicycle."

I nodded and smiled awkwardly. I guessed she was right. I was probably the young man with the bicycle. In any case, I was relatively young and used a bicycle for most of my journeys. I could also answer to being a foreigner with a goatee, living on the ground floor.

After I had been identified there was silence in the hallway. The two women looked at me with questioning eyes. I guessed it was time for me to explain my presence here on the upper floors of the apartment building.

"I'm returning the underwear to the woman in apartment 5-3," I said and raised my hand holding the underwear so that the women could see it.

As the words left my lips I realized that they had not come out quite right. They could be misinterpreted. I felt myself blushing. The hallway was silent again and the women waited for me to explain my case further.

"Err, I mean. Err. The underwear fell off the clothesline," I managed to stutter. "I found it on my patio."

"It's the dark haired woman with the dog," the somewhat younger woman with the bathrobe told the old woman with the wonky wig.

"Huh?" replied the old woman with the wonky wig.

"It's the dark haired woman with the dog who owns the underwear," explained the somewhat younger woman with the bathrobe.

"Oh?" replied the old woman with the wonky wig who did not seem to be completely understanding the situation.

"Yes, the dark haired woman with the dog dropped her underwear while putting out the laundry and it fell down on to the patio of the young man with the bicycle."

The old woman with the wonky wig nodded. She appeared to be starting to understand the mystery behind my presence here on the upper floors. I was relieved to know that the confusion had been resolved and it was time for me to head back downstairs. I said goodbye and waved to the two women – perhaps inappropriately – with the same hand that was holding the underwear.

"Give me the underwear," said the somewhat younger woman wearing a bathrobe and grabbed the underwear from my waving hand. "I will give it back to the dark haired woman with the dog."

I would have preferred to deliver the laundry to

its rightful owner without the aid of middle men – or rather – without the aid of the somewhat younger middle woman wearing a bathrobe. Yet I did not know if it was appropriate to ask the somewhat younger woman with the bathrobe to give the underwear back to me. Hence, I said goodbye and returned downstairs. My job here was done. The somewhat younger woman with the bathrobe would return the underwear to the – so-called – dark haired woman with the dog.

★ ★ ★ ★ ★

I was startled upon hearing the doorbell ring. I crawled off the sofa and turned off the TV. Apparently I had fallen asleep during the news. I headed for the door and opened it. Outside was a dark haired woman with a dog.

"Evening. I'm your neighbor in apartment 5-3," said the dark haired woman with the dog.

"Uh-huh," I yawned and thought that this must be the dark haired woman with the dog.

"I dropped some laundry on to your patio."

Right! I was not sure how I should react to that. I did not know how to start telling her that I did not have her laundry anymore.

"I don't have it," I said knowing that it was not a sufficient explanation but not knowing how to continue.

"Huh?" The dark haired woman with the dog seemed surprised. This needed some more explanation.

"The woman in apartment 5-2 has it," I answered blushing. If only the somewhat younger woman with the bathrobe had not taken the underwear.

"Huh?" The dark haired woman with the dog did not quite follow. Who can blame her? This was a complicated situation. If only I knew how to explain it further. I did not know if she understood who I was referring to, but I could not think of any way to describe the somewhat younger woman with the bathrobe in more detail. Obviously, I could not refer to her as the woman with the bathrobe since I guessed it was quite a coincidence that she had been wearing a bathrobe when I met her.

"The woman with the bathrobe?" asked the dark haired woman with the dog.

Exactly! The dark haired woman with the dog had solved the case. Apparently, describing her as the woman with the bathrobe would not have been inappropriate.

"Exactly!" I replied, happy that the situation was becoming clearer.

"Why does the woman with the bathrobe have my underwear?"

Good question. The situation was perhaps not becoming as clear as I had hoped. It still needed some clarification.

"She took it," was the only thing I could think of.

"She took it?" replied the dark haired woman with the dog.

"Err, yes. She took it." How could I explain it more clearly?

"From the patio?" asked the dark haired woman with the dog.

"No, from my hands."

"Why was my underwear in your hands in front of the woman with the bathrobe?" asked the dark haired woman with the dog. Her surprise seemed to be turning into anger. Who could blame her? It was a complicated situation.

"I took it upstairs. You were not at home. She came out. She snatched it from my hand and said she would return it."

Now we were talking. That had not been so difficult, had it? I was happy that I had finally managed to explain what had happened.

"But she is weird!" the dark haired woman with

the dog said after thinking about my explanation for a while. I did not know how to reply. She lowered her head to look at the dog.

"Why is my underwear in the hands of the woman with the bathrobe?" asked the dark haired woman with the dog. I did not know if she was still talking to me or had started talking to the dog. "Why her? She is weird! Just as weird as the old woman with the wonky wig. But not as old."

I did not know what to say. I was not even sure if she was talking to me anymore. Her anger seemed to have changed into hopelessness. She went silent. I remained silent.

"Well. I guess that's it," the dark haired woman with the dog said as she looked up from the dog to me.

"I guess that's it," I replied.

That was indeed it. The dark haired woman with the dog said her goodbyes and called the elevator. I said my goodbyes and closed the door. As I headed back to the sofa I passed the mirror. I stopped and looked at my own reflection and said: "So you really are the young man with the bicycle."

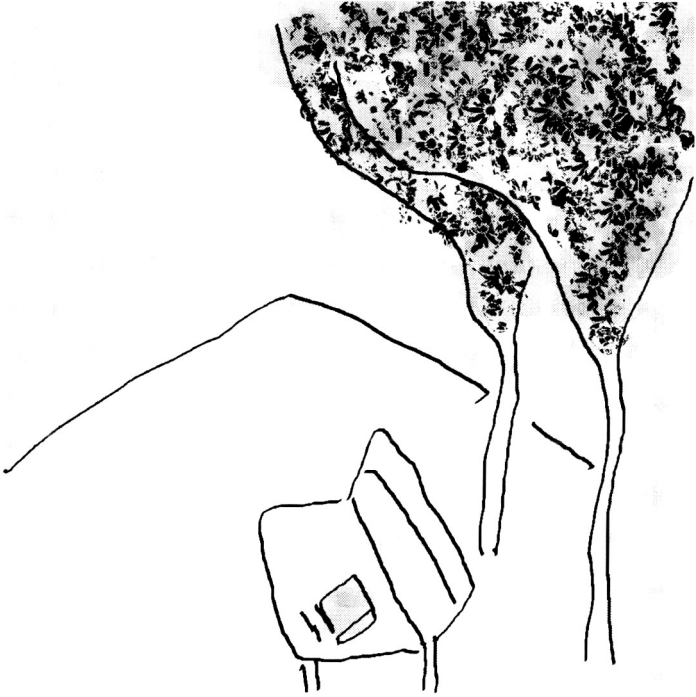

THE PEOPLE IN THE SQUARE

It was a Sunday morning in early August and the sun
was high in the sky. I walked slowly along Carrer
de Congost. I stayed on the side of the street where
I could use the shade of the surrounding buildings to
shield me from the sun. I passed the bar run by punks
and squatters. Across the street was the headquarters
of the Gràcia homing pigeon breeding society. I smiled
at the idea that such opposites could co-exist in this

small Barcelona street. On one side was an association with the dove as their symbol – the symbol of peace. On the other side was an association with a skull and crossbones as their symbol – the symbol of terror. On this quiet Sunday morning the only signs were of peace and terror living together in peace and harmony.

At the end of Carrer de Congost I turned left and then right again into Carrer d'Astúries. I was on my way to Virreina square. My favorite square in the Gràcia neighborhood. The square where I sat so often at weekends with a book in my hand, which was sometimes accompanied by a pen.

Once in the square I found myself a seat on a bench in the shade of a tree. The square was lively and yet at the same time it radiated tranquility. The terraces of all three cafés were fully occupied by customers whose murmur echoed around the square. On all the benches in the square there were people. Some were reading. Some were engaged in lively discussions with their bench-mates. Others sat in silence watching life as it evolved in the square. The life in the square evolved slowly in the August heat. People were careful not to move too fast in order to make the heat more bearable.

The church stood in all its glory on the mountain side of the square. As in other parts of the world there are four cardinal directions in Barcelona. Contrary to other parts of the world they are not called north, south, east and west. The cardinal directions in Barcelona are mountain, beach, right and left. The church door stood open. His kingdom is always open. Especially on Sundays.

There was a constant stream of people walking across the square. People walking their dogs. People on their way home with the sunday paper under one arm and a baguette under the other. Tourists – a middle-aged man and a woman – walking with a map in their hands. "Look! There is the church that we saw in the Barcelona tourist guide." They stopped and took a photo before walking on in search of the next square. In search of the next item they had seen in the Barcelona tourist guide.

The pigeons flew back and forth across the square. They sat down on a ledge above the church door before flying over to the next tree. Their next stop was the facade of a house on the beach side of the square. The pigeons finished their circuit by flying back across the square to the ledge above the church door. Every now and then they came down to earth to look for breadcrumbs left over by the wingless occupants of the square. A young and inexperienced pigeon walked up to a cigarette butt. It realized immediately that the butt was not edible and walked over to the next butt to try its luck there.

I pulled a notebook and pen out of my breast pocket. I had the intention of trying to write a short story. I had not written anything for a long time. I was suffering from writer's block. Whenever I sat down with the intention of writing, my head went blank and I could think of nothing worthy of putting onto paper. I had turned to the square in the hope that the fresh air would help me air out my brain and blow in fresh ideas.

I stared at the empty pages in the notebook in front of me. Barcelona, August 9th 2008, I wrote on the top of the left sheet. I got no further. I did not know what to write. I put the notebook in my lap and looked around me. I watched the two drunkards who sat on a bench across the square discussing life's mysteries between taking sips from the cans of beer they had in their hands. They laughed. They were joyful. Their life was no bed of roses but who needs a bed of roses when one always seems able to scrape together enough coins to buy the next round of beer.

"You never put any money into the household," I heard someone say behind me.

I turned around slowly and looked at the people

sitting on the bench behind the one where I was sitting. There was a young couple with a small baby. They were not joyful. They were not sitting and admiring their baby as so many young parents do. They were arguing. They were paying no attention to the baby. The baby was paying no attention to them. It slept quietly in its mother's arms.

"I have enough with taking care of the baby. All my money goes into taking care of the baby. You know that. I have tried to ask mom for more money but she refuses to give me more. She says that I should be grateful that she sends me any money at all."

"Why don't you tell her about the baby? Why don't you tell her you have had a baby and you have two people to care for?"

"Never!" the girl cried. She blushed with embarrassment and looked around her before looking at the baby to see if it had woken up. The baby slept. The girl lowered her voice and continued the discussion. "I cannot tell her about the baby. She would go mad. She would probably stop sending me money."

"But what about your dad. He has buckets full of cash. Why don't you ask him for money?"

"You know why. We have been through all this before. He has renounced me. He has never forgiven me for quitting my studies and moving to Barcelona."

The young couple did not get any further with their discussion about the household budget. The baby woke up and started crying. The girl stood up. "Let's go!" she said. "I need to go home to feed the baby." I watched the young couple disappear behind one corner of the church.

From behind that same corner a jogger appeared. He paid no attention to the young couple with the baby. He was preoccupied with his own set of problems. He jogged through the middle of the square away from the church. At the other end of the square he took some time to make up his mind about where to go next, before turning right into a side street. This was the first time he had gone running since he had moved to Barcelona. He was completely lost. He looked to be facing a long run if he did not run into a familiar looking sight soon.

At the next corner he ran into an unfamiliar looking sight. He had run into a young woman. She recovered quickly form being run over and walked rapidly across the square as fast as her feet could carry her. She was way too late. She had promised her friend to help her clean her apartment. She was two hours late. She had gone out last night. She had planned to go home early.

She had planned to get an early night. She didn't. The night out had gone on long into the night. She had got home very late. She had woken up late.

She felt embarrassed about letting her friend down. Her friend had done nothing that could justify such a betrayal. She hoped her friend would not get angry. She hoped her error would be forgiven. She walked quickly across the square as fast as her feet could carry her. She was way too late. She was embarrassed. She was worried. She was oblivious to the fact that her friend had also gone out last night, had also gone to bed late, and was still sleeping.

Hugo had gone to bed early and woken up early. He was now sitting on the terrace of one of the cafés reading a business newspaper. He wondered how he could make a profit from buying and selling stock. This was the third consecutive weekend that he had thought about the same issue. He had thought it would be easy. He had thought he could simply buy stock at a low price and make a profit by selling it at a higher price. He was about to discover that trading stock was not as simple as that. Over the last three weeks that he had been reading the business newspaper he had noticed how the price of some stock rose while the price of others fell. He had found no pattern in the movement of the price. It made him hesitant to start trading. He was afraid to lose quickly the small sum of money he had put aside for his stock trading adventure. He decided to abandon his idea of stock trading. He decided to use the money to buy himself a new camera. Who knew? Maybe he could make some money from selling photos.

Pedro had worked as a photographer all his life and earned enough to bring home the bacon – along with an occasional leg of ham. Now, he walked slowly across the square together with his wife María. They were old and it took them a while to walk across the square. Gone were the days when they raced across the square. Their square. They had played in the square when they were children. Their first kiss had been on the steps of the church. Pedro had proposed in the square. María had said yes in the square. They had got married in the church in the square. They had bought their first and only apartment in the square. Their children had taken their first steps on the square. Their children had chased after their first pigeons in the square. Even after their children had grown up and left their parents' house, they frequently visited the old couple with the grandchildren. On these occasions there was a feast in the square. Now, Pedro and María were so old that they had time to reflect on the highlights of their life while they walked across the square.

"Look!" I heard someone cry to my left. "We are wearing identical shoes."

I turned my head. I recognized the woman who was sitting beside me. She was one of the drunkards in the square. I saw her almost every time I was in the square. At first I had not realized that she was one of the drunkards. I had thought she was just a crazy old lady. Later I noticed her drinking together with the other drunkards. She was crazy for sure. Whether it was from old age or booze I did not know. I looked at her feet. I looked at my feet. We were both wearing sandals. Sandals as different one could imagine.

"Yes," I said to the old lady and smiled. "You are right. We are wearing identical shoes."

I turned the pages in my notebook and browsed back to the page where I had written Barcelona, August 9th 2008. A few densely written pages had been added to my collection of writing. I closed the book. I put the pen in my pocket. It was time to go home. I said goodbye to my sandal twin. I said goodbye to the square. I said goodbye to the people in the square and thanked them for the inspiration they had given me. I thanked them for the story fragments I had been

able to put on paper today. I doubted any of the fragments would ever grow into a standalone story. That
was however of no importance. The only thing that
mattered was that I had started writing again. I could
head home, content with the day's labor.

ABOUT THE AUTHOR

Name: Börkur Sigurbjörnsson
Address: Spain, 999 Abroad

Börkur Sigurbjörnsson was born in Reykjavík in the year of the dragon 1976. Börkur has a PhD degree in computer science from University of Amsterdam. He currently lives in Barcelona where he works on Web related research and development, along with writing fiction.

999 Abroad is Börkur's first literary publication and is a collection of shortstories that have appeared on the Urban Volcano over the past few years. The title comes from the Icelandic Registry and refers to the default values for the postal-code and city used in the registration of Icelandic citizens living abroad.

Links

Web: http://borkur.net/
Stories: http://urbanvolcano.net/
Twitter: @borkurdotnet

2465547R00050

Printed in Great Britain
by Amazon.co.uk, Ltd.,
Marston Gate.